Beverly Lewis

Beverly Lewis Books for Young Readers

PICTURE BOOKS

In Jesse's Shoes • *Just Like Mama*
What Is God Like? • *What Is Heaven Like?*

THE CUL-DE-SAC KIDS

The Double Dabble Surprise
The Chicken Pox Panic
The Crazy Christmas Angel Mystery
No Grown-ups Allowed
Frog Power
The Mystery of Case D. Luc
The Stinky Sneakers Mystery
Pickle Pizza
Mailbox Mania
The Mudhole Mystery
Fiddlesticks
The Crabby Cat Caper
Tarantula Toes
Green Gravy
Backyard Bandit Mystery
Tree House Trouble
The Creepy Sleep-Over
The Great TV Turn-Off
Piggy Party
The Granny Game
Mystery Mutt
Big Bad Beans
The Upside-Down Day
The Midnight Mystery

Katie and Jake and the Haircut Mistake

www.BeverlyLewis.com

THE CUL-DE-SAC KIDS

No Grown-ups Allowed

Beverly Lewis

BETHANY HOUSE PUBLISHERS
MINNEAPOLIS, MINNESOTA 55438

© 1995 by Beverly Lewis

Published by Bethany House Publishers
11400 Hampshire Avenue South
Bloomington, Minnesota 55438
www.bethanyhouse.com

Bethany House Publishers is a division of
Baker Publishing Group, Grand Rapids, MI

Printed in the United States of America by
Bethany Press International, Bloomington, MN

ISBN 978-1-55661-644-0

Library of Congress Cataloging-in-Publication Data
Lewis, Beverly.
    No grown-ups allowed / by Beverly Lewis.
        p.   cm.—(The cul-de-sac kids ; 4)
    Summary: Jason takes advantage of his parents' absence to
sneak forbidden chocolates behind his babysitting grandmoter's
back, but a Bible verse and a talk with God help him understand
the importance of good behavior.
    ISBN 978-1-55661-646-9 (pbk.)
    [1. Candy—fiction. 2. Grandmothers—fiction. 3. Christian
life—fiction.] I. Title. II. Series: Lewis, Beverly. Cul-de-sac kids ;
4.
PZ7.L58464No   1995
[Fic]—dc20   96-023931

Cover illustration by Paul Turnbaugh
Story illustrations by Barbara Birch

17 18 19 20 21 22 23   33 32 31 30 29 28 27

This book is dedicated
in loving memory
to
my grandmother,
Zelma Elaine Jones.
(1906–1994)
Her chocolate chip cookies
were the best
in the world,
because she mixed them
with love.

THE CUL-DE-SAC KIDS

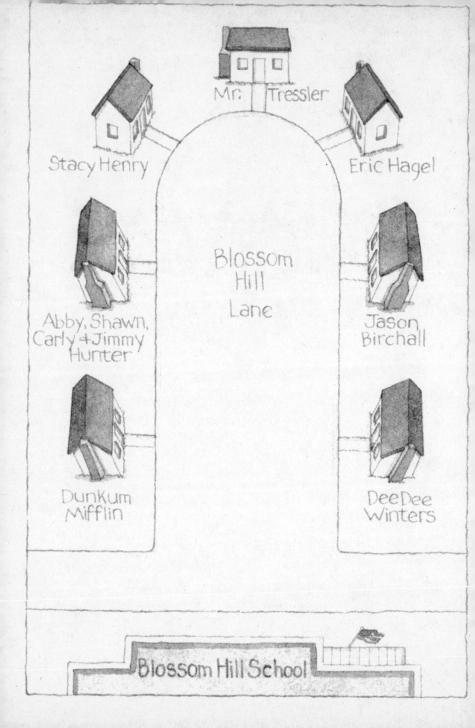

ONE

Jason Birchall stared at the valentine box on the kitchen table. He could almost taste the juicy chocolates. Cherry-filled, jelly-filled, coconut . . .

"Jason," his mother called. "Come here, please."

He backed away from the heart-shaped box. He didn't want his mother to know what he was thinking. Snitching thoughts!

"Coming," Jason answered.

His mother sat on the sofa in the living

room. "Let's talk," she said.

But Jason's mind was on something else. He was thinking about ooey gooey chocolates.

"We're going out of town for Valentine's Day," his mother began. "And Grandma Birchall will stay with you from Friday until Sunday."

Jason whined, "Oh, Mom. A whole weekend with Grandma?"

His mother frowned. "Now, Jason, you know better than that. Your grandma will take good care of you."

Jason quickly changed the subject. "Can't I stay up late on Friday night?"

His mother shook her head. "You must get your rest, Jason. It's important."

"But, Mom!"

"Jason," she said firmly. "You will go to bed at your regular time. I don't want you to be sick."

Jason nodded, but he didn't mean it. He was tired of taking pills. He was tired of being an Attention Deficit kid. No junk food and early bedtimes were boring. It was time for a change—a big change.

Jason tiptoed to the kitchen. He glanced over his shoulder. Was his mother watching? Could she hear him lift the candy box lid?

The glorious smell greeted his nose. Ah, yes! Jason's taste buds started to jig. They danced the chocolate twist, followed by the ooey gooey chocolate boogie.

The fantastic smell floating out of the valentine box grabbed Jason. It made him pick out the juiciest mound of chocolate. It made him plop that mound into his mouth.

"Jason Birchall!"

He jumped half out of his skin. Slowly, he turned around. There stood his mother. She glared at him, her hands on her hips.

Jason gulped.

11

TWO

Jason nearly choked. *She must have come in during the chocolate boogie,* he thought.

He tried to speak. "Yesh?" The heavenly ball of chocolate crowded his mouth.

His mother scolded, "I can't turn my back for one second!"

Jason swallowed. The sweet mound of heaven slid down his throat. Five seconds was too short to enjoy a chocolate valentine.

"Well, Jason?" his mother asked.

"I'm sorry." But Jason was only sorry about one thing—the short time the chocolate stayed in his mouth.

Mrs. Birchall opened the lid. The smells leaped out of the box. She counted the chocolates. "How many did you eat?"

"Just one."

She stared at the heart-shaped candy box, then at Jason. "Are you sure?"

Jason nodded.

"You *know* what sweets do to you, Jason."

But Jason didn't care about being wound up and hyper. He could think of only one thing. Dark, rich chocolate.

His mother snatched up the pink valentine box. "I'll put this away." And she carried it out of the kitchen.

Jason peeked around the corner. He watched her turn into the master bedroom. He heard the closet door squeak open.

Good! Jason could almost see the hid-

14

ing place. It was the same spot his parents hid Christmas candy. And caramel corn. And Dad's M&M's.

Just then, the garage door opened. Jason ran to meet his dad.

"Here's an early Valentine's Day gift," his dad said. He handed the gift to Jason.

Jason tore the wrapping off and looked at the present. It was a tiny marker board with a green marker.

"Like it?" his dad asked, smiling.

"Uh, sure, thanks." Jason stared at the gift. *Just what I always wanted,* he thought.

"You can write important things on it," Dad explained. "It will help you remember to take your pills while we're gone."

Jason pulled the green marker off the Velcro. He wrote his name on the board. His stomach felt tight. He gritted his teeth. His parents were no fun. No fun at all! Why did God make parents anyway?

Jason followed his dad into the house.

He shuffled down the hall to his room. Closing the door, he plopped down onto his beanbag.

Jason drew a picture on his new marker board. It was a giant ice cream sundae. Covered with chocolate candies. And gobs of whipped cream.

He daydreamed about the chocolates in his mother's closet. He thought about his plan. Soon he wouldn't have to daydream about chocolates. He would gobble them right down!

Jason took his glasses off and twirled them. He danced a wild jig. Friday—two days away. He would trick his grandma. Easy!

THREE

At last it was Friday.

Jason walked home with the Cul-de-sac Kids. All the kids lived on Blossom Hill Lane. Seven houses on one cul-de-sac.

"My grandma is spending the weekend," Jason told his friend Dunkum.

"Sounds like fun," Dunkum said.

"No kidding!" Jason said.

Dunkum stopped in the middle of the street and stared at Jason. "What's *that* supposed to mean?"

"Nothin' much." Jason ran and slid on the snow.

Abby Hunter tossed her scarf around her neck. "I think Jason is up to something!"

Dunkum nodded. "I better have a talk with Jason's grandma."

Dee Dee Winters giggled. So did her best friend, Carly Hunter—Abby's little sister. "I *like* your grandma," said Dee Dee.

"Me too," said Carly.

Stacy Henry laughed. "Who needs a sitter when you're in third grade? I stay by myself every day after school."

"But what about for a whole weekend?" Abby asked.

"Guess you're right," Stacy said. "That's too long to be alone."

Abby's Korean brother, Shawn, threw a snowball at Stacy. It bounced off her backpack.

"Why you!" Stacy dropped her stuff

18

and reached down. She pushed a pile of snow together. "This is war!" she shouted, giggling.

Eric Hagel grinned. "You're in for it now, Shawn!"

The kids watched Stacy smooth out her snowball. She added more snow to it, then patted it hard. She tried to pick it up. It was too heavy.

Shawn marched into the snowy street. "I help you, Stacy. This make good snowman." He spoke in broken English because he'd just come to America. Shawn and his brother Jimmy had been adopted by Abby's parents.

"Goody!" shouted Carly. "Let's build a snowman."

"How about a snow monster?" Eric suggested. "The biggest one in the world."

"Make him an alien!" yelled Jason.

"There's no such thing," Abby said.

"So what," said Jason. "There aren't any monsters, either." But he thought

19

about his plan to trick his grandma. Now *that* was something a monster might do!

The kids took their school stuff home and came back with buckets of warm water.

"Let's make him in *my* yard!" Jason hollered.

Just then Grandma Birchall stepped outside. She stood on the porch, waving to Jason.

Jason looked the other way. On purpose. He knew what she wanted. It was time for his medicine.

"Jason, dear," she called.

"In a minute," Jason snapped. Then he ran to help Eric and Dunkum roll up a huge snowball. They grunted as they pushed it across the yard.

Abby and Stacy made a medium-sized ball.

Dee Dee and Carly made the head. Carly started laughing.

"What's so funny?" Abby asked.

Carly kept giggling. "We could call the snow creature Dino-Dunce. And give him a walnut-sized brain."

"I know! He could have a tiny head like a Stegosaurus," Dee Dee added.

Eric laughed. "Who said anything about making a dinosaur?"

"Yeah," said Jason. "What happened to our alien?"

"Let's mix him all up," suggested Dunkum.

"Yes!" Shawn shouted. "We make snowman-monster-dino-alien."

"And let's call him our February Snow Creature," said Abby.

"Our what?" Stacy asked.

"You know, like at the Winter Carnival in Minnesota," Abby said. "My grandparents took us to see it once."

"Yes!" said Shawn. "We make great snow creature." He and Jimmy, his little brother, were grinning.

Jason couldn't remember seeing

Shawn and Jimmy so excited. Except for the day Abby and Carly's parents adopted them. That was Thanksgiving—three months ago.

Jason had an idea. "We could rope off the cul-de-sac and charge a fee to see our snow creature."

"For how much?" Dunkum asked.

"Enough for an ice cream party," yelled Jason.

"You're not supposed to have sweets," Dee Dee reminded him. She wrinkled up her nose.

Jason gritted his teeth. He'd have sweets if he wanted to. He was thinking of his mother's valentine chocolates this very minute.

Jason turned and looked toward his house. *Good!* Grandma had gone inside. *She's probably making supper,* he thought. *Now is a good time to sneak inside. Nothing can stop me now!*

23

FOUR

Jason crept onto the porch and tiptoed inside. Grandma was tinkering around in the kitchen. All clear!

First, he sneaked down the hall. Then he dashed into his parents' bedroom.

Squeak! He slid open the closet.

There were hatboxes and shoe boxes on his mother's side of the closet. Color coded as always. Red was for dress up. Blue was for work at her beauty shop. Green was for around the house. Everything was in order.

Now for the candy!

Jason pushed his father's shirts aside. Behind them was a shelf for belts and ties and things.

Before he could see the box, Jason smelled the chocolates. His taste buds shivered. They quivered.

Dark, rich chocolate balls! Waiting to melt into pools of sweet bliss in his mouth.

He reached for the box and opened it. The fattest candy seemed to call his name. Jason placed it on the end of his tongue.

"Gotcha!"

Jason whirled around. He stared into Abby Hunter's face.

"Spit it out!" she said.

"You cwavy?" Jason said, his mouth full.

Abby shook her head. "Say what you want, but we need those outside." She was giggling now as she grabbed the candy box. She held up two plump, juicy choco-

26

lates. "What *bee-u-tee-ful* eyes you have!"

Jason stared at his friend. He couldn't believe it. She was going to use his mother's chocolates for snow creature eyeballs!

Jason chewed up the gooey candy and swallowed.

Abby waved her finger at him. "Does your grandma know what you just ate?"

"Do I look *that* dumb?" Jason said.

Abby raised her eyebrows. Then she turned and ran out of the house. But Jason was right behind her.

"Jason, is that you, dear?" It was his grandma calling from the kitchen.

Oops! Jason froze in his tracks. "Uh, yes, Grandma, it is."

She came into the living room wearing an apron. It was tied in a bow around her trim waist. "Come here, dear. I need a hug." She held out her arms.

Jason hugged her, but held his breath so she wouldn't smell the chocolate on his breath.

"It's time for your medicine, young man." She pulled a bottle of pills out of her pocket. Opening the lid, she put one in Jason's hand.

Jason spun around and hurried out the door.

Grandma called after him, "Do you want a glass of water, dear?"

"Not this time," Jason yelled. And as soon as she wasn't looking, he dropped the pill into the snow. *Poof!* It disappeared.

There! Grown-ups can't tell me what to do! Jason decided. He felt mighty good about taking charge of things. His way.

FIVE

Jason helped Shawn and Jimmy pour water on the snow. They rubbed out the bumps so the snow would harden. Nice and smooth.

Jimmy found an old twig and snapped it in two. "Snow Creature . . . funny arms," he said.

Stacy found another twig. "Here, this girl needs three arms."

"GIRL?" shouted Jason.

Stacy grinned.

Dunkum frowned. He plopped his blue

hat on Snow Creature. "There, now it's a BOY!"

Dee Dee ran home and came back with two pieces of lettuce for ears.

Abby licked the pieces of chocolate. *Smack!* She stuck them on Snow Creature's face.

Jason gritted his teeth. *What a waste!*

The kids clapped. It was perfect, except for one thing. The nose.

"Is SHE a snooty snow creature?" asked Stacy, looking down her own nose.

"No, HE needs an antenna nose," announced Eric.

"Let's have a nose vote," said Abby. "How many want Stacy's idea?"

Stacy, Dee Dee, Carly, Abby . . . and little Jimmy voted yes.

"No fair!" Jason whined. "Jimmy can't vote with the girls."

Dunkum whistled. "Here's a freaky idea. We'll give S.C. two faces, one on each side of his head."

"S.C.?" asked little Jimmy. He looked confused.

"Santa Claus, right?" Jason said, laughing.

The boys cheered.

"Hey, wait a minute," said Abby. "Don't get Jimmy all mixed up. S.C. stands for Snow Creature."

"S.C. need two heads," Jimmy said.

"Yes!" Shawn said. He began rolling up another snowball.

"A two-headed snow creature," said Stacy. "One for the boys; one for the girls!"

"Ours will look beautiful," bragged Dee Dee.

Eric strutted around Snow Creature. "But ours will be better!"

Abby frowned. "This isn't a contest. We're the Cul-de-sac Kids—we stick to-gether, remember?"

Dunkum grinned. He marched up to Abby and stood beside her. "The president of the cul-de-sac is right."

So the kids set to work, for the fun of it. And by dark, Snow Creature was finished.

The head created by the boys wore Dunkum's blue knit hat. Black olives made the eyes. And a red rubber band formed the mouth.

The head created by the girls wore Abby's straw hat. Red licorice formed the mouth. And lettuce made the ears. Two chocolate eyeballs stared straight at Jason's house.

Jason wished the chocolates were melting in his mouth. Instead of freezing rock hard outside.

"Time for supper," Grandma Birchall called.

Jason hurried to the front porch. He turned to look at Snow Creature once more. HE was terrific!

Inside, Jason smelled Grandma's meatloaf and potatoes. He ate some of everything. Grandma smiled when he finished.

Boy, did I fool her! She thinks I'm full, Jason thought as he planned his dessert. Ah, dessert! The rest of the valentine chocolates, of course.

The truth was he shouldn't have chocolate at all. And he knew it. Chocolate made him very hyper, sometimes sick.

Grandma stacked the dishes on the counter while Jason went to the living room. He sat on the sofa waiting for his big chance. Dessert was calling.

Click! Jason turned on the TV with the remote control. He found channel 7 and leaned back. It was a loud, shoot-'em-up cop show.

Grandma peeked around the corner. "Is that something your parents let you watch?" she asked.

"Every night."

"Jason, are you sure?"

"Uh-huh," Jason lied.

At the commercial, Grandma came in with a cup of coffee. Quickly, Jason switched to the news channel.

Grandma settled into a comfortable chair and watched. "This looks interesting," she said, sipping her coffee.

Jason stared at the coffee in Grandma's cup. The dark color reminded him of valentine chocolates—the ones in his mother's closet!

Grandma seemed interested in the local news. So Jason sneaked out of the living room and made a beeline for the hallway.

It was now or never!

SIX

Jason found the valentine box and stuffed it under his shirt. He dashed across the hall to his room.

Whoosh! He slid under his bed on his stomach. Grandma would never find him here. Under the bed, he opened the lid. One after another, he ate the chocolates. Mm-m! It was chocolate heaven at last.

After the sixth one, Jason's taste buds rolled over and played dead. He couldn't taste a thing!

Then something strange began to happen. Jason felt shaky all over. Like he could jump up and down and never stop!

He tried to get out from under the bed, but he bumped his head on the box springs. He tried to slide out backward. His foot was stuck in the bed frame coils. He rocked back and forth.

Crash! His head hit the bed. "Ouch!" he yelled. Jason was trapped. But he couldn't lie still. Inside, his whole body wanted to move. Like tiny grasshoppers dancing and twitching.

He pushed the valentine box aside. *No more, no thanks!*

Now Grandma was calling. Jason stared at the half-eaten candy box. The ooey gooey chocolates smelled horrible. Besides that, he had a stomachache.

Jason was in big trouble. He hadn't taken his afternoon pill—the pill that helped calm him down. His body needed that medicine.

"Jason," his grandma called again.

"I'm here," whispered Jason, still under the bed.

He was too sick to shout.

"Jason, I dished up some fruit for dessert."

He pushed away from the box springs, trying to get his foot unstuck. He rocked. He rolled. He wiggled.

Bam! The bed frame came loose on one side. It fell on top of him.

"HELP!" It was easy to scream now. Jason kept howling till Grandma showed up.

"Oh, my dear! My dear!" Grandma lifted the bed frame off poor, sick Jason.

Free at last, Jason jumped up. "You saved me. I could've been framed forever."

Grandma scratched her misty gray head. "Are you all right?" Then her eyes grew narrow. She studied him. "You're all chocolaty." The smudges on his face told his secret.

Grandma pointed Jason toward the

39

bathroom. "Let's get you washed up, young man."

He plodded off to clean his face. But when he closed the door, he forgot why he was there. That often happened when he didn't take his pills.

Jason pulled a plastic bag down from the cabinet. It was full of cotton balls. One by one, he lined them in a row on the sink counter top.

Soon Grandma was knocking on the door. "Are you all right, dear?"

Jason looked in the mirror. Oops! A chocolaty face stared back. Gooey spots smeared his glasses.

"Jason?" Grandma called again.

"Uh, just a minute." He turned on the faucet. It was hot water. Too hot, so he added cold. *SWOOSH!* The water splashed over the sink, onto the floor.

"Jason!" Grandma sounded upset.

"I'll be right out," Jason grumbled. He leaned over the sink and cupped his hands under the faucet. He rubbed them over his face, spreading the chocolate all around.

Just then, another idea struck. Jason plugged up the sink and floated cotton balls in it. Two handfuls of them.

Grandma called again, "I'm coming in!" The bathroom door swung wide. "What a mess you've made," she said, and began to clean up.

Jason dried his hands on his jeans. Things had gone crazy. But it was still only Friday. *Plenty of time left before Mom and Dad come home,* he thought.

Friday night! Monster movie night! Jason was dying to see a monster movie. His first ever.

If only he could get rid of the ache in his stomach. If only he could get Grandma to go to bed early!

But how?

SEVEN

Jason jigged down the hallway to the living room. He plopped into his dad's favorite chair. Holding his stomach, he groaned.

Grandma came in looking worried. "Let's get some warm tea in you." She touched his arm. "Come in the kitchen, dear."

Jason wasn't paying attention. He reached for the TV section of the paper instead. Something caught his eye. A sale at the pet store—tomorrow!

Jason read the ad. *VALENTINE SPE-CIAL: FROGS AND LIZARDS HALF PRICE.*

A frog! For as long as he could remember, Jason had wanted a frog. He would do anything for one.

He dropped the newspaper. "Grandma, can we go downtown tomorrow?" He turned on the charm. "Please?"

"If you behave yourself, we'll see about it," she said from the kitchen.

Jason burst out laughing. "It's a deal!" But, of course, he had no plans to behave. And he would wait to tell Grandma about the frog.

"Your tea is ready," Grandma said.

Jason hurried to the kitchen. "I'll clean up the kitchen for you," he said. Jason wiggled all over waiting for her answer.

"What a dear boy," Grandma said. She pulled out a chair for him. Then she served him a cup of mint tea. Stirring in a little honey, his grandma smiled. "We're

44

VALENTINE
SPECIAL

FROGS & LIZARDS

½
PRICE!

having a lovely time together, aren't we?"

Lovely? Jason rubbed his stomach and groaned. "I feel horrible," he said.

"Sip your tea slowly," Grandma said. "It will help."

Jason held his breath and pretended to sip and swallow. "I'm done." He pushed the cup away.

Grandma frowned at him over her glasses. "Perhaps an early bedtime will help."

"After I do the dishes," he said. "And you can watch TV while I do that." He was hoping she'd get sleepy and go to bed early.

"Why, thank you, dear," Grandma said, heading for the living room.

Jason turned on the water at the sink. Next came dish soap. He squeezed out too much, and it made tons of bubbles. Soon, they were dripping down the sides of the counter. And onto the floor.

Jason was getting more and more hyper. His last pill had been at breakfast.

His mother had placed it beside his hot oatmeal and toast. Right in front of his nose.

When Jason finished in the kitchen, it was messier than when he started. He held his stomach as he went to his room. *It's too early to go to bed,* he thought.

Peering out the window, he saw lights across the street. Abby and Carly Hunter and their Korean brothers were still up. And Dunkum's lights were on next door. Stacy Henry's, too.

"All the Cul-de-sac Kids are up," he muttered. "It's only 7:30." Shoving the curtains closed, he planned his next move.

He hopped like a frog over to his closet and pulled out his robe and pajamas. "Er-r-rib-bit!" he croaked over and over. Then he got undressed.

His plan was perfect! Now if he could just stay awake till Grandma went to bed.

EIGHT

Grandma tucked Jason in and gave him a kiss on the forehead. "Sleep well, dear," she said.

"Good-night, Grandma," he whispered, pretending to be tired.

"I think I'll read awhile. It's early. If you need anything, I'll be across the hall in your parents' room."

"Thanks, Grandma." Jason wanted to sound polite. More than that, he wanted to trick his grandma. Late-night TV was on his mind. Once she was asleep, he would get up.

Jason listened to the clock in the hall. He counted the ticks, but he couldn't lie still. At last, he sat up in bed. Was Grandma asleep yet?

Tiptoeing across the hall, Jason peeked into the room. His grandma was sitting up in bed, but her eyes were shut. And a book lay open on her lap.

Yes! Jason closed her door softly and dashed to the living room. He lay on the floor in front of the TV. Some scary show was on. He could tell by the music.

Jason gritted his teeth as a giant snowman roared down from the mountain. It had a monster face.

A snow creature? thought Jason. *Nah, couldn't be.*

Suddenly the music changed. It got louder and higher in pitch. Jason turned down the volume. He didn't want Grandma to wake up.

Phooey on grown-ups! thought Jason.

He sat close to the TV. The giant snowman clumped down the mountain and across the field. It was heading straight for two boys. They were shoveling snow.

Jason watched, eyes glued to the screen. What was the snow giant going to do? Why didn't the boys turn and run?

Jason held his breath. *Yikes!* His stomach knotted up as the snow giant crept behind the boys.

Leaping up, Jason stood in the middle of the living room. The snow giant roared and the boys ran for their lives. Jason's muscles felt frozen. His breath came in short puffs as he watched the boys run. Jason wished they'd hurry. The snow giant was catching up with them.

"Hurry! Get away," Jason said to the TV.

Just then—*cre-eak!*—Jason's front door inched open.

Jason jerked around, ready to fight off the snow monster. "NO!" he yelled as a furry hand touched the doorknob.

Jason's heart did a giant flip.

NINE

"Anybody home?" It was Dunkum. He stomped his feet on the mat. "It's freezing out there."

"Don't you ever knock?" Jason asked.

"I did," Dunkum insisted.

"I didn't hear you," Jason replied. He pointed to the TV screen. "Check this out."

Dunkum sat on the sofa for a minute, then he frowned. "I don't watch scary stuff."

Jason wasn't listening now. He was

watching the snow giant bend the boys' shovels in half.

During the commercial, Jason stretched. "What are you doing here?" he asked Dunkum.

Dunkum grinned. "I'm checking up on you."

"I'm fine," Jason said.

Dunkum got up and looked in the kitchen. "It's a mess in there. Where's your grandma?"

"What do you care?"

Dunkum frowned. "You can't fool me, Jason Birchall." He pulled something out of his pocket. "Look what I found in the snow."

Jason stared at it. It was his afternoon medicine. The pill he should have taken. "Hey, where did you get that?"

"From the pill fairy," Dunkum teased.

Jason held his hands up like a boxer.

Dunkum dodged Jason's swing.

"Whatcha doin' Sunday morning?"
Dunkum asked.

"Me?"

"You and your grandma," Dunkum
said.

"Not much," Jason said.

"Why don't you come to church?
There's room in Abby's van." Dunkum
turned to leave.

Jason remembered the Christmas ser-
vice at Dunkum's and Abby's church. The
ushers had given out candy. Maybe they'd
have valentine candy *this* Sunday!

"Sure, I'll come," Jason replied.

"Good." Dunkum's eyes sparkled. "It's
a special day. We're having a kids' choir."

Jason liked music. It made him want
to dance. Slow or fast, it didn't matter.
"That's good," he said, but the commercial
was over now. And the snow giant was
back.

Jason hardly heard his friend say
goodbye.

At the next commercial, Jason tiptoed to his room. He pulled the chocolates out from under his bed. Time for a little snack.

By the end of the movie, Jason wished Dunkum had stayed. They could have shivered together with fear. But Dunkum was smart. He didn't watch this stuff.

It was late and Jason was wiped out. He jumped into bed without washing his face or brushing his teeth. He held his stomach. It was hurting again. But not as bad as the pain in his head.

He shook all over and scooted under his covers. Jason glanced at his clock. The time glowed back at him. It was past midnight!

The room was darker than usual. It made Jason nervous. If he stared into the blackness long enough, little snow creatures began to appear.

E-eek! Jason hid under the covers. But he couldn't hide from the snow giant's roar. It was stuck in his brain. It made him quiver and quake.

Suddenly, Jason heard another sound. Low at first. Then it grew louder. He reached for the light. Dashing to the window, Jason cupped his hands on the frosty glass.

The two-headed snow creature shimmered under the streetlight. One set of eyes stared back at him—the chocolate ones.

Jason bumped his head on the window. He blinked. "What's going on?" he whispered.

Snow Creature moved his twig arms.

Jason rubbed his eyes.

Then it happened again!

Thump! Thump! Jason's heart pounded in his ears. *Had Snow Creature come to life?*

TEN

Whoosh! Jason closed the curtains. "Grandma!" he hollered.

She rushed into the room. "What is it, dear?"

Jason danced around, trying to tell her what he'd seen. "It started with a low roar. I looked out the window. That's when I saw him move!"

"Please slow down, Jason. What are you saying?"

"It's Snow Creature. He's alive! Look outside!"

A sleepy smile spread across her face. "You must be dreaming."

Jason tugged on her nightgown. "Come see for yourself."

"You can't see anything outside with this light on." She flipped the switch off.

Jason stood at the window. "Just watch," he whispered.

The two of them waited. And waited. The snow creature stood very still.

At last, Grandma tucked Jason in bed again. "It must be all those chocolates you ate," she said. And she blew a kiss.

Jason shook all over. There was a live snow creature out there making roaring sounds. Just like in the movie. And Grandma was going back to bed!

Not Jason. He reached for a book from his shelf. It was a Christmas gift from Abby Hunter. It had a Bible verse and a story for each day of the year.

Jason pulled his knees up to his chin and read: *Children, obey your parents in the Lord, for this is right. Honor your father and mother . . . that it may go well with you and that you may enjoy long life on the earth.*

Jason stopped reading. He thought about things going well if he obeyed his parents. He wanted to live a long time on the earth. And he thought about obeying. *That* was hard.

Next, he read the story. It was so good, he forgot about being scared. The book from Abby had done the trick. Nothing could scare him now. He turned the light out and fell asleep.

Hours later, Jason heard a noise at his window. He sat up in bed. There it was again.

Someone was knocking on his bedroom window!

Jason was too tired to care. Maybe he was dreaming. He hoped so. Then he could snuggle down into his blankets again.

SCR-I-I-TCH! SCR-A-A-TCH!

Jason leaped out of bed. He peeked between the curtains. His heart jumped.

Snow Creature was staring into his window. He had walked all the way across the yard!

Jason dashed away from the window, yelling for Grandma. She *had* to believe him now. Jason raced across the hall. Running up to the bed, he pulled the covers down. The bed was empty!

Jason ran out of the room and down the hall. "Grandma!" he called.

He opened the front door and ran out into the night. He looked around. Snow Creature was still standing beside his window.

Jason darted back inside and slammed the door. His heart thumped wildly.

Suddenly, he had an idea. He would go outside and tell off that Snow Creature! Who did he think he was, scaring him like that?

Jason pulled his coat on over his pajamas. He shook with fright. What if Snow Creature had gotten to Grandma's room first? What if he had taken her away?

Jason ran through the house shouting, "Grandma! Where are you?"

Grandma was nowhere to be found!

ELEVEN

At that moment, Jason missed the grown-ups in his life. His dad, his mom, and his grandma . . . all of them. He was on his own now. Alone with scary Snow Creature!

He took a deep breath and opened the front door. He stared at Snow Creature. A mean look shot out of the icy monster's eyes. Jason shivered.

And then it happened. A low roar bellowed out of Snow Creature's mouth.

Yikes! Jason wanted to run inside. But

no! He was determined to be brave. Marching up to Snow Creature, Jason punched his snowy stomach.

"You're not alive," Jason shouted. "This must be a bad dream."

Snow Creature took a giant leap toward him.

But Jason stood still. "All I have to do is pinch myself and you'll be back where you belong," he shouted. He pointed to the spot where he and the Cul-de-sac Kids had made the creature.

"That's what *you* think," Snow Creature thundered, reaching out to grab Jason. "Your grandmother is mine now. And you are next!"

"No! No!" screamed Jason. He twisted away from Snow Creature's reach. "No!"

★ ★ ★

"Jason, dear! Wake up! It's Grandma."

He twisted and rolled around in his sheets.

66

"You're dreaming," Grandma said.

Jason opened his eyes. The sweetest wrinkled face in the world smiled down at him. He rubbed his eyes. "Nobody should watch scary shows," Jason whispered. "Not ever."

His grandma nodded slowly. "It's almost time for breakfast," she said. "And your pill."

Jason started to groan but stopped.

"Maybe you won't have to take pills when you're a grown-up," she said.

Grown-up. A nice word, thought Jason.

Grandma went to fix scrambled eggs and toast. Jason could almost taste it. A good breakfast beat chocolate candy any day!

At the table, Jason took his pill. And after breakfast, he brushed his teeth and washed his face.

Jason went to his room and wrote on his marker board.

67

Always remember—

1. *Take pills*
2. *Watch good TV shows*
3. *Go to bed early*
4. *Obey grown-ups (like parents and grandparents)*

Jason spotted the book from Abby. He remembered the verse about obeying your parents. Then, kneeling beside his bed, Jason talked to God. He was sorry about watching the scary movie. And about eating his mother's chocolates. He was sorry about not wanting any grown-ups around.

After the prayer, Jason hopped around his room like a frog. He pretended his bed was a lily pond.

When Grandma peeked in, he shouted, "Er-rib-bit! For-give-it?"

She sat on the bed. "That's an interesting word."

"Oh, Grandma, I'm sorry I didn't obey

you. I got out of bed and watched a scary monster movie and . . ."

"I know you did, dear," she said calmly.

"You do?"

Grandma nodded. "You didn't expect me to sleep through all that roaring, did you?"

Jason grinned. He should have known. "Well, I'm sorry. And that's the truth."

"It was a hard lesson," Grandma said. "And goodness me, what scary music!" She put her hand to her forehead.

Jason gave her a big squeeze. "Oh, Grandma, I love you!"

★   ★   ★

Later that night, Jason fell asleep thinking about his visit to the pet shop. And his half-priced frog—a valentine gift from Grandma.

But when he dreamed, it wasn't about frogs. Or scary snow monsters. It was about grown-ups. Grown-ups like his mom and dad.

And tomorrow, they were coming home!

THE CUL-DE-SAC KIDS SERIES

Don't miss #5!

FROG POWER

Stacy Henry hates frogs—especially Jason Birchall's new bullfrog, Croaker. But when she plans an Easter pet parade for the Cul-de-sac Kids' parents, guess who gets stuck measuring Croaker for his bow tie! Can Stacy master her fear of frogs in time for Easter? Or will she create disaster in the cul-de-sac?

ABOUT THE AUTHOR

Beverly Lewis doesn't eat much chocolate, but her husband and three kids do. Cuddles, their cockapoo dog, snitches chocolates when no one is looking.

Beverly has fun with pets—real and pretend. She features them in all her books. Muffie pulls a puppy prank on J.P. in MOUNTAIN BIKES AND GARBANZO BEANS. In THE SIX-HOUR MYSTERY, a guide dog named Honey senses danger at school before the fire alarm sounds!

Look for lots of pets in THE CUL-DE-SAC KIDS series!

Also by Beverly Lewis

Adult Nonfiction

Amish Prayers
The Beverly Lewis Amish Heritage Cookbook

Adult Fiction

HOME TO HICKORY HOLLOW
The Fiddler • *The Bridesmaid* • *The Guardian* • *The Secret Keeper* • *The Last Bride*

SEASONS OF GRACE
The Secret • *The Missing* • *The Telling*

ABRAM'S DAUGHTERS
The Covenant • *The Betrayal* • *The Sacrifice* • *The Prodigal* • *The Revelation*

ANNIE'S PEOPLE
The Preacher's Daughter • *The Englisher* • *The Brethren*

THE ROSE TRILOGY
The Thorn • *The Judgment* • *The Mercy*

THE COURTSHIP OF NELLIE FISHER
The Parting • *The Forbidden* • *The Longing*

THE HERITAGE OF LANCASTER COUNTY
The Shunning • *The Confession* • *The Reckoning*

OTHER ADULT FICTION
The Postcard • *The Crossroad* • *The Redemption of Sarah Cain*
October Song • *Sanctuary** • *The Sunroom* • *Child of Mine**
The River • *The Love Letters* • *The Photograph* • *The Atonement*
The Wish • *The Ebb Tide*

Youth Fiction

Girls Only (GO!) Volume One and *Volume Two*[†]
SummerHill Secrets Volume One and *Volume Two*[‡]
Holly's Heart Collection One[†], *Collection Two*[‡], and *Collection Three*[†]

www.BeverlyLewis.com

---

[*] with David Lewis   [†] 4 books in each volume   [‡] 5 books in each volume